For Mom and Dad

Published in the United States by Random House Children's Books,
a division of Random House, Inc., New York, and simultaneously in Canada
by Random House of Canada Limited, Toronto.
www.randomhouse.com/kids

Library of Congress Cataloging-in-Publication Data
Woods, Noah.
Tom Cat / written and illustrated by Noah Woods.
p.   cm.
SUMMARY: Tom Cat is not sure he is a cat at all, preferring to pretend to be a cow, a pig,
or even a bat, until the day he utters a "meow" and discovers that it feels pretty good.
ISBN 0-375-82497-9 (trade) — ISBN 0-375-92497-3 (lib. bdg.)
[1. Identity—Fiction. 2. Cats—Fiction.] I. Title.
PZ7.W8643To 2004 [E]—dc21 2003001005

MANUFACTURED IN MALAYSIA First Edition 10 9 8 7 6 5 4 3 2 1
RANDOM HOUSE and colophon are registered trademarks of Random House, Inc.

TOM
CAT

WRITTEN AND ILLUSTRATED BY

NOAH WOODS

Random House 🏠 New York

This is Tom.

Tom is not your average cat.

From the moment he was born,

his mother and father knew

their Tom Cat was a little different.

Frankly, Tom wasn't even sure

he was a cat!

Instead of making sounds

like the other cats,

Tom would say . . .

"Cats love to chase mice,"
his parents explained.

"Then I must be an elephant!"
Tom said.
"Mice scare me!"

"I will climb a tree
and build a nest,"
Tom decided.

"Usually, dear boy,"
his parents said,
"birds build nests."

"I must be a bat!"
Tom said from above.

"Please come down,"
his father called out.
"I'm pretty sure you're a cat."

"Ple-e-e-e-e-e-a-s-s-s-e, Tom,"
his mother said,
"come out of the mud."

"I think I might be a pig!"
Tom replied.

"You've been in
  the bath all day!"
  Tom's mother said.

"I'm probably a duck,"
  Tom replied.

"Why are you jumping
up and down, Tom?"
his father asked.

"Maybe I'm a kangaroo!"
Tom said.

"Snails leave trails, Tom,"
his father pointed out.

"Really?" said Tom.

"Then I must be a snail!"

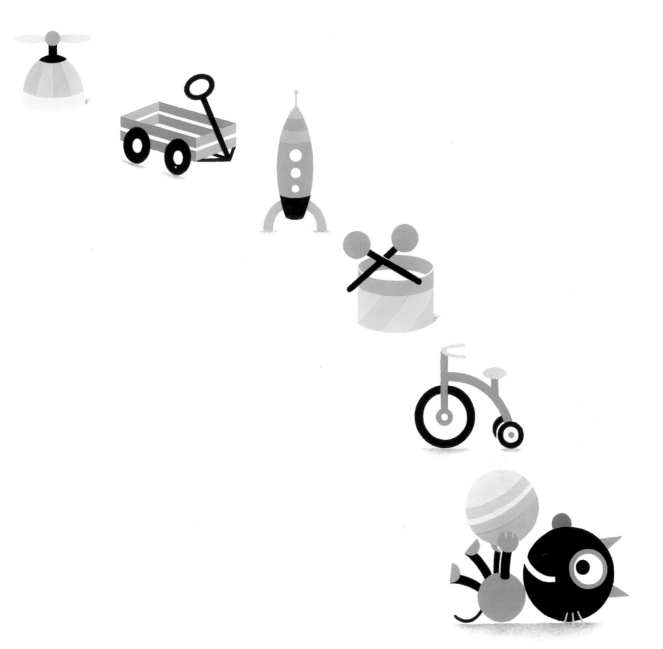

"Do you think
  I might be a chipmunk?"
  Tom asked.

"No, dear," his mother said.
"There's really no need
  to store food in your cheeks."

"Maybe," Tom thought out loud,
"I'm the black sheep
  of the family!"

"No, Tom,"
  his parents replied.
"You are the black *cat*
  of the family. "

"Are you sure I'm a cat?" Tom asked.

"Sometimes you call me a little tiger . . .

and sometimes you call me a silly goose."

"You *are* a little tiger,"
Tom's parents said.
"And sometimes you *can*
be a silly goose!"

"But mostly you're
a little pussycat."

"Usually, Tom,"
   his parents said,
"*cows* jump over the moon.
   But even if you think you're a pig,
   a duck, or a cow,
   we love you no matter
   who you are."

One day, out of the blue,
Tom made an unexpected noise.

"Meow," he quietly said.

"What was that?" his mother asked.

"Meow!" Tom said again.

"Where did *that* come from?"
his father asked.

"I really don't know," Tom replied.
"All of a sudden, it just came out
and it felt really nice.
I think I'll do it again."

"I didn't know I could do that!"

"I don't think I can stop!"

"It just rolls off my tongue!"

"Meow! Meow! Meow!"

"I must be a cat after all!" Tom said.

"Gee whiz!"
said a mouse.
"You sure make
a lot of noise.
I liked it better
when you said,
'Quack! Quack!'
How about a 'moo'
or a 'cock-a-doodle-doo'?"

"Sorry!" Tom said.
"I just can't do it.
I was meant to 'meow'
and I can't hold back!"

"I . . . am a cat!"

Now Tom even chases mice.

Moo!
Arf!
Oink!